I'm bored!

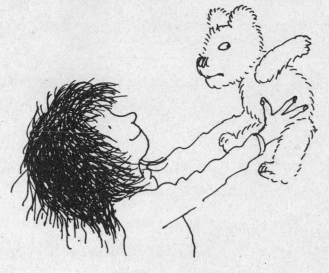

BEL MOONEY

I'm bored!

illustrated by **Margaret Chamberlain**

mammoth

For Toby Prior, a very brave boy
B.M.

First published in Great Britain 1997
by Methuen Children's Books Limited

This edition first published in 2001 by Mammoth
an imprint of Egmont Children's Books Limited
a division of Egmont Holding Limited
239 Kensington High Street, London W8 6SA
for The Book People Ltd
Hall Wood Avenue, Haydock, St Helens WA11 9UL

Text copyright © 1997 Bel Mooney
Illustrations copyright © 1997 & 2001 Margaret Chamberlain

The moral rights of the author and illustrator have been asserted

ISBN 0 7497 2921 X

1 3 5 7 9 10 8 6 4 2

A CIP catalogue record for this title
is available from the British Library

Printed in Great Britain
by Cox & Wyman Ltd, Reading, Berkshire

Contents

I want something to happen

Kitty thought that all this was a very bad idea. It wasn't fun at all. In fact, she thought it was one of the worst things ever.

Mum was very, very fat. She reminded Kitty of one of those funny toys you hit and it just rolls back into place with a silly grin on its face.

Only Mum wasn't grinning at all. She was usually in a bad mood, or else she

was tired. It wasn't much fun. What's more, Kitty was fed up with Dad taking her on one side and telling her to be a good girl.

Good girl? Kitty knew she wouldn't be Kitty if she was a good girl. Her cousin Melissa was a good girl and nobody liked her very much. Still, Dad whispered to her that she must think about Mum and not herself, and so on. Because Mum was having a baby.

That's what Kitty thought was a very bad idea indeed.

One day it all got too much for Kitty. Mum was lying on the sofa watching television. Dad had made her a sandwich, but he had also made a mess in the kitchen – which he asked Kitty to clean up.

'But I'm going to play Frustration with Dan,' Kitty protested.

'No, you're not — I've got some homework to do,' Dan said, and went upstairs.

'Boring goody-goody!' yelled Kitty.

'Don't disturb Mum,' said Dad

'You play with me, Dad, pleeeeeeese,' begged Kitty.

'Sorry, Kit, I've got to put the clothes in the washing-machine,' said Dad. 'Now be a good girl.'

'That's boring!' wailed Kitty.

But she went into the kitchen and did the washing-up — making a lot of noise so that everybody would know how good she was being. She got the cloth and wiped the crumbs off the table. Most of them fell on the floor, but Kitty didn't care.

'I'm really bored,' she muttered.

When Kitty was bored it was as if a curtain came down inside her head. She couldn't think what to do, so she got more bored. The only thing to do was to be very naughty — because then something was happening. Then Mum and Dad and Daniel took notice of her, which was what Kitty wanted.

So, without really, really meaning to, Kitty dropped a mug. It was a very old mug, one Mum didn't like. It made a lovely crash.

Dad came rushing in. 'Oh, Kit — what have you done?' he asked.

Kitty grinned. 'I dropped it,' she said.

'I can see that,' said Dad.

He picked up the pieces, so that Kitty wouldn't cut herself. While he did that, Kitty was busy pouring salt on the table, spreading it out and making pictures in the salt with her fingers. It was fun.

'Stop making that mess, Kitty!' said Dad, when he saw what she was doing.

'Well, what else shall I do. I'm bored!' whined Kitty.

'Go and paint a picture,' said Dad.

'My paints are all mucky,' said Kitty.

'Well, go and read,' said Dad.

'I've finished my library book,' said Kitty.

'Well . . . er . . . make something,' said Dad.

'What with?' asked Kitty. Then she added in a hopeful voice, 'You could take me out and buy me some Plasticene!'

'No – you know I want to stay here with Mum,' frowned Dad.

'Well, I'll just have to go on being bored, won't I?' said Kitty.

'Being very boring, more like it,' Dad shouted, and slammed out of the kitchen.

After a few minutes Kitty wandered upstairs and lay down on her bed. She held Mr Tubs and whispered all her troubles into her teddy's ear.

'It's not fair, Mr T,' she said. 'Mum is always tired because of this baby, and Dad only thinks about Mum, and Daniel won't play with me, and I'm FED UP!'

She thought she heard Mr Tubs grunt, but she couldn't be sure.

'I just wish something would HAPPEN!' wailed Kitty.

She thought she saw Mr Tubs close his eyes for a second as if he was very sleepy, but she couldn't be sure about that either.

Dad said she was boring. Maybe that was true. Maybe Mr Tubs was so bored being with her that he wanted to go to sleep. Sure enough, her teddy bear flopped on his side, with his back to her.

'I wish something would happen!' Kitty sighed, and in a few minutes she fell fast asleep too. She was having a lovely dream about a party given just for her by Rosie, William, Anita, and all the others in her class. They gave her presents and let her win all the games, and it was lovely to be the centre of attention. 'Kitty! Kitty!' they called as the exciting parcel landed in her lap . . .

'KITTY! KITTY!' somebody was shouting – and this was real, not a dream.

Her bedroom door was flung open and there was Dan. He looked very worried, but excited too.

'Get up, Kit!' he said.

'Why?' asked Kitty.

'Something's happening – Mum's started to have the baby! Quick! Dad's taking her to hospital and we've got to go next door to William's house until Auntie Susan can pick us up. It's all arranged . . . Oh, Come on, Kit!'

Kitty followed her brother downstairs, to find Dad helping Mum on with her coat. Mum had one hand on her big tummy. The little suitcase was by the front door. They both looked very pink and pleased, although Dad was hopping from one foot to the other in the rush.

'Bye, pet,' whispered Mum, giving Kitty a big hug.

Suddenly Kitty wanted to cry, and she

clung hard to Mum. 'Can't we come with you?' she asked.

'You know you can't!' said Mum. 'But you can come and visit me very soon. Then there'll be a lovely surprise!'

'*Please* let's go!' said Dad – and the next minute they were off.

Daniel and Kitty went through the gap in the fence to William's house. Dan was excited but Kitty felt very worried.

'I wanted something to happen – but I didn't want this to happen,' she said in a very small voice.

'We're going to have a new baby!' crowed Dan.

At William's house everybody was

excited. William's Mum and his sister Sally chatted on about whether the baby would be a boy or a girl, and Daniel and William both said they knew it would be a boy.

'Why?' asked Kitty.

'Because we couldn't stand another girl like you, Kitty!' grinned Daniel. That made everyone smile.

Kitty glared at them all and felt terrible. The truth was, she was worried about Mum and a bit scared about all this baby business. But she couldn't show it. So she had to frown and be the same bad old sulky Kitty.

She asked, 'How long do we have to wait, then?' in a very cross voice, as if she was bored stiff. In fact, she did think it was very odd that nobody seemed to know how long babies took to arrive. After all, you knew when a train would come, didn't you?

The waiting seemed to go on for ever. They watched television, and ate sandwiches William's mum made, and wondered when Auntie Susan would come and get them. It was horrible.

A few hours later the phone rang. Kitty jumped, and they all listened as William's mother made squeaky noises. She put the phone down at last and turned to the children with a big smile.

'Well – that was quick!' she said. 'Kitty and Dan – your Mum's had the baby already! She's really well and happy, and everything's fine!'

Kitty felt this huge weight lift inside her chest. She'd been so very worried and now everything was all right. It had happened – and Mum was fine. Kitty was so happy she wanted to cry.

'Have we got a boy or a girl?' Dan shouted.

'A little brother!' said William's mum.

Daniel and William both yelled, 'Hurray!' but Kitty wouldn't let them them get away with that.

'Oh no!' she groaned, leaning over and pretending to be sick.

'Oh, Kitty, what's wrong now?' asked William's Mum.

They were all looking at Kitty, waiting.

'Boys are so BORING!' she said.

Baby Tubs

It was four weeks since Baby Thomas was born, and the house had changed for ever. There were little white blankets, cardigans and bootees everywhere, and tiny coloured all-in-one suits hanging on the washing-line.

The pram filled the hall, and the cot took up the space by Mum's bed – where Kitty used to climb in, sometimes, in the mornings. Through the day there would be very noisy times when the baby would cry and cry and cry, until Kitty thought his little red head would cry itself off his shoulders.

Then there would be times when Mum said, 'Shhhh!' and Kitty had to tiptoe around and talk in a whisper. That was very difficult indeed.

The worst thing was that Mum and Dad and Daniel seemed to have gone a bit mad. Kitty would come across one of them hanging over the cot or the pram or the rug on the sitting-room floor where Thomas kicked his legs.

'Whoos a sweetie? Whoos Dada's darlin' ickle diddums baby boy, then?' cooed Dad.

'Such a little preshus . . . such a boofulbabba,' whispered Mum.

'Helloo Tomtom! Helloooooo lickle Tomtom!' giggled Daniel, waggling his fingers in the baby's face.

It was all very silly.

Of course, Kitty did like the new baby. He was very sweet, with his bald head, sticky-out ears, button nose and little, round, toothless mouth. But everybody made such a fuss of him, all the time,

that Kitty felt quite left out.

She knew that was why she felt so
strange, but knowing the reason didn't
help. She wanted to be Mummy's baby,
and that wasn't possible any more.

One day she went over to William's
house to see if he wanted to play, but he
and a boy from school called James were
kicking a football around the garden.
Kitty joined in for a while, but she soon
felt bored. They didn't want her to play

– she could tell. So, feeling left out, she came home.

Then she rang Rosie's house – and found out that Rosie had gone over to Anita's for the day.

Why didn't they ask me? Kitty thought – and felt even more left out.

What could you do when life seemed so flat? Kitty looked at all her toys and they bored her, even the castle that had once seemed so magical. Her paints were dirty, the fuzzy felts seemed babyish, her crayons needed sharpening, the Plasticene was all mixed up and she needed some new . . .

What can I do? thought Kitty.

She heard Mum's voice and wandered across the landing to her room. Mum was bending over the changing pad, where a pair of little, fat, pink legs waved in the air. Baby Thomas had no clothes on. Kitty peered at him and giggled, because she felt a bit embarrassed.

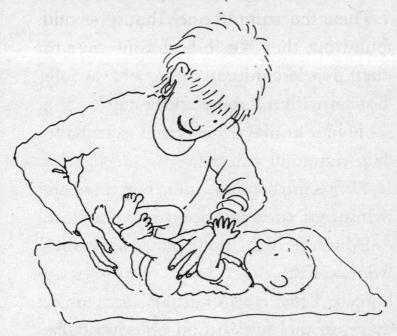

'What is it?' asked Mum.

'He looks rude,' said Kitty.

'No he doesn't, he looks *lovely*,' said Mum, in that soppy voice, turning the baby over to powder his bottom. Kitty stared and didn't think he looked lovely at all.

She watched as Mum got the disposable nappy and its plastic cover, and started to put it on Tom. Then the little vest, then the blue all-in-one suit, then a little cardigan and a blue woolly bonnet with a bobble on the top.

'He looks like a fat parcel,' said Kitty, but Mum didn't hear.

'Who's my beautiful baby boy, then?' she whispered, cuddling Baby Thomas close.

'Mum – will you play with me?' whined Kitty.

'No, Kitty, I'm putting Tom in his pram in the garden and planting bulbs. Why don't you come out and help me?'

'Gardening's boring,' wailed Kitty. Mum shrugged and walked out, carrying the baby.

Later, looking down from her bedroom window, Kitty could have kicked herself. It would have been fun messing about in the soil with Mum. The sun was out, the baby was asleep in the pram, and Mum was bending over the flowerbed with a trowel in her hand. Kitty knew she could have made herself really dirty and not been told off.

But the bad Kitty had spoken, and now she couldn't go out and say sorry. She couldn't. When you've been bad you need a sort of excuse to be good again . . .

Kitty looked helplessly around her room and spotted Mr Tubs lying on the floor with his bottom in the air. Without thinking she picked him up and cuddled him close. Whenever she felt lonely and unhappy Mr Tubs was there. She could tell him everything, and he always gave her good advice. It's true! Inside her head Kitty always seemed to hear Mr Tubs talking and telling her what to do.

'Who's my beautiful bear then?' whispered Kitty, in a Mummy-type voice.

Mr Tubs looked cross and growled that he wasn't a baby.

'Oh yes you are! You're *my* baby,' said Kitty, 'Mr Tubs, you're so clever you're a genius!'

She took her teddy through to Mum's bedroom, and laid him down on the changing pad. Soon there was talcum powder all over his fur, but that didn't matter. It made him smell just like baby Tom . . . when his nappy was clean, of course!

It took longer than Kitty expected. The disposable nappy was easy, but it took a lot of fiddling to get the little vest on, as Mr Tubs was too fat. Then it took even longer to cram his tubby arms and legs into the red and white striped all-in-one suit. Then Kitty hunted around and found a clean white cardigan in Mum's baby drawer. She put some blue bootees on him for good measure. Finally she pulled a white bonnet over his ears — which stuck out under it like two lumps.

'Der! Whoos mumma's ickle bearikins?' cooed Kitty.

Mr Tubs looked very funny — and very cross indeed. Kitty laughed and laughed as she picked him up in just the way Mum picked up Baby Thomas, with one hand under his bottom for support.

She opened the back door and walked out into the garden, very slowly, as if she was carrying a real child. Mum glanced up and for a second she was taken in – since, from behind, Mr Tubs looked like a lumpy little parcel of baby, just like Tom.

'Who . . . ?' she began, looking puzzled.

Then Kitty got closer and turned him round. Mum dropped her trowel, rocking back on her heels and laughing as if she would burst.

'Can I put my baby in the pram too, Mum?' asked Kitty.

Mum got up, still laughing and took Mr Tubs from Kitty. 'What have you done? Oh, Kitsy,' she spluttered, 'I think your baby's even more beautiful than mine!'

They sat Mr Tubs in the bottom end of the pram, where Tom's feet didn't even reach. He looked very funny peering

over the end, wearing the bonnet, and
with talcum powder on his nose.

'I think they'll both sleep now,' said
Mum, 'so shall you and me steal some
time together, KittyKat?'

'Yes please, Mum,' beamed Kitty.

The rainy day stories

It was half-term and the drizzliest, greyest, dankest, dimmest holiday Kitty could remember. Most of the leaves had fallen from the trees but Christmas seemed such a long way off. The rain poured and poured, as if the sky had got so unhappy it just couldn't stop crying.

Mum was busy with the baby (of course) and Dad was at work (of course) and Daniel had gone out to a friend's house and wouldn't take Kitty (of course). So Kitty sat at home and looked at the raindrops chasing each other down the windowpane, and decided they were having a better time than she was.

Kitty wanted some fun! She shouted to

Mum that she was going to William's house.

Kitty was just going out the back door with no coat on when Mum yelled to make sure she was wrapped up. Kitty sighed. Why was it you always knew what grown-ups were going to say?

She threw her anorak over her shoulders, and set off down the garden and through the gap in the fence. She got a bit dirty, but didn't care. At William's back door, though, his mum looked cross.

'Take your shoes off, Kitty,' she said. 'They're all muddy.'

Kitty sighed and did as she was told. Why was it that sometimes all mums seemed the same?

William was watching TV – or at least, he wasn't *watching* it, he was flicking the remote control and surfing the channels.

'Hi, Kit,' he said, in a flat sort of voice, without looking at her.

'Will – shall we do something?' said Kitty.

'I'm watching TV,' said William.

'No you're not. It's really boring flicking about,' said Kitty. 'You're not following anything.'

'Well, I can't think of anything else to do,' said William.

'We could play Snakes and Ladders,' Kitty suggested, hopefully.

'Nah – that's boring,' said William.

At that moment Kitty decided she hated William and went home without saying goodbye. She didn't even put her anorak on when she crossed the rainy garden, she felt so cross with everyone.

Back in her own house she decided to phone her friend Rosie, to see if they could make a plan.

'Aw, Kit, it's too wet to come out,' said Rosie.

'So what are you doing?' Kitty demanded.

'Watching TV,' sighed Rosie.

'That's not doing *anything*!' Kitty shouted, and put the phone down.

Next she rang Anita. She hoped she might be invited round to Anita's house, because she always liked it there. But Anita said she was helping her mother make naan bread.

'Can I come and help?' asked Kitty.

'Well, actually, we've just finished. So Mum's going to clean up.'

'What are you going to do?' asked Kitty.

'Watch TV with my little brothers,' said Anita. 'Mum says I've got to keep them out of her way.'

'Don't talk to me about little brothers,' growled Kitty, her heart sinking. She wandered around the house, picking things up and putting them down, until her Mum (who was sitting peacefully feeding the baby) said, 'Please, Kitty, will you stop fiddling and go and do something!'

'I DON'T KNOW WHAT TO DO!' wailed Kitty.

'Ohhh . . . er . . . put the television on,' said Mum in desperation.

That did it. Kitty looked at the television sitting in the corner of the room and suddenly saw it as a square, grey monster, the colour of all the human brains it gobbled every day. It seemed to like children's brains especially – nasty, greedy thing! She thought that if it was sick bits of all the children would pour out into the room . . . YUK!

They had to be saved.

Kitty would be Batgirl and fight the forces of evil.

But how?

She looked out of the window at the rain drumming on the roofs, and suddenly it gave her an idea. Quickly she phoned Rosie, then Anita, and told them she was having a rain party.

'A rain party?' said Rosie.

'What's a rain party,' asked Anita.

Kitty told each of them they'd have to wait and see. She knew that would get them out of their armchairs and on the way to her house! Next she went to Mum and told her she had to cure all her friends of their rainy day boredom. Of course, that would mean she had to raid the cupboard where Mum kept crisps and biscuits, and be allowed to make a flask of warm blackcurrant juice.

Mum said yes. Then Kitty had to rush around making preparations, until at last she was ready to carry everything to the

special place she had thought of.

William, Rosie and Anita arrived at the time Kitty had said, all wearing anoraks and boots. They looked excited. Kitty hoped they wouldn't be disappointed by what she had planned. But, surely anything was better than watching TV all day!

'Don't take your coats off,' said Kitty, 'we're going outside!'

She led the way down the garden to the little, wooden garden shed at the bottom. Kitty liked the shed. It smelt of soil and damp, and was full of interesting things like gardening tools and rolls of green twine. Today it was even more interesting, because Kitty had laid out the food and drink on a clean tea towel on a box in the middle of the floor, and arranged stools and boxes for them to sit on.

It was quite dark inside the shed because it was such a dull day. The rain drummed on the roof, sounding very loud.

'This is the rain den,' said Kitty, 'and don't worry, it'll soon warm up with us all in it.'

'But what are we going to do?' asked Rosie, looking quite excited.

'Play the rainy day story game,' said Kitty.

On the table, with the crisps and biscuits, she had put four piles of rough paper and four pencils, and there were four cups with bits of paper in them.

'Now,' said Kitty, 'we each have to take a piece of paper from each cup. When you've got all four, you look at them, and there's a word on each. Then you have to make up a story.'

'With just four words?' asked William.

'No, stupid! You just have to include

the four you've got.'

'Can the story be about anything?' asked Anita.

Kitty said yes.

'Great!' said Rosie, with a big grin.

Kitty held out the cups, and soon each of them had four bits of paper. Kitty told them all to look and she did the same. Soon the shed echoed to loud groans which drowned out the rain.

'It's so hard!' wailed Anita.

'Everybody read theirs out,' crowed Kitty. 'I bet you mine are the worst – so I'll start. I've got RAIN, WITCH, ANGRILY and THIN.'

'I've got FOG, TV SET, SLOWLY and BAD,' said William, giggling.

'Mine are SUN, PIG, SLEEPILY and PRETTY,' smiled Rosie. 'I'm glad I've got 'sun'.

'And I've got SNOW, FAIRY,

QUICKLY and LITTLE,' said Anita.

'Will you swap?' asked William. 'I think yours are easier than mine.'

'No swapping,' said Kitty firmly. 'We've all got ten minutes now to write the story. Then we'll read them out – so they've got to be good!'

'They've all got weather in them!' Rosie pointed out.

'That's because it was on my mind,' nodded Kitty.

'Is there a prize?' asked William.

'You get some food!' Kitty said, pointing at the crisps and biscuits.

There was silence in the shed as the four children chewed their pencils, looked at the ceiling, fiddled with ears and hair, shuffled their feet, made little moaning noises . . . then started to write. It was warm and cosy with the rain pattering on the roof.

Kitty closed her eyes. That way she thought the stories wouldn't know she was there, and so come creeping up into her mind. It usually worked. Her pencil scratched on the paper. She looked up, and her three friends all looked busy. She decided she had been very clever. At last she looked at her watch and cried, 'Time's up!'

'Mine's no good,' moaned Anita.

'Rubbish!' said Kitty.

Everybody looked pleased, but a bit nervous at having to read out what they had written. William went first, then Anita, then Rosie, and Kitty last. They clapped each other's stories as if it had been a proper competition, and then ate the food, drank the juice, and talked and talked. When Kitty suggested a game of I Spy (because the shed was full of odd things) nobody said no. And the time whizzed by – until at last Kitty's Mum appeared in the door. The rain had stopped, but it was nearly dark.

'It's time to come in now, kids,' she smiled.

'Mum! We've written stories, and had a much better time than watching TV, and, and . . . you've got to guess who wrote which one!' shouted Kitty.

'It'll be easy!' said Rosie.

So they swapped about and

read the four little tales to Kitty's mum, who sat down on a box to listen. When she heard each one she guessed who had written it – and do you know, she she was right each time.

Do you want to hear the rainy day stories? I have put their spelling mistakes right!

William's story
I went out into the FOG and I couldn't even see my feet. I thought a ghost or a baddie would come and get me and I was frightened. So I started to run down the road faster and faster until I was flying right above the fog. Then, SLOWLY, it started to clear but I could still fly and so I flew all over the town shouting, 'Look at me.' Soon I went over my own house and saw that the sitting-

room window was open. I dived through and went right into the front of the TV SET and into the Superman film that Dad and Mum and Sally were watching. And I really was Superman, but they didn't know it was me in there. But all the BAD people did, and now they were frightened of me! So there!

Anita's story

Once upon a time there was a SNOW FAIRY who came down at Diwali when all the houses are full of lights and we have sweets and presents. The snow fairy went to visit a LITTLE girl called Anita Attra who lived in Melton Road but who was sad because she had never seen real snow – only a bit last year. So the snow fairy made a spell and Anita QUICKLY fell asleep. The fairy took her to the North Pole where they had lights in the whole sky for Diwali and all the ground was white. Then the fairy showed Anita how to make a snowman, and took her in a sledge, and they played snowballs until it was time to go home. Anita woke up in her own bed, but guess what? Her hands were all cold and wet.

Rosie's story

My granny lives in Jamaica where the SUN shines nearly all the time, but she is staying with us now. She tells me stories about the village where she lives and especially about her PIG called Jumba. Jumba has lots of piglets all the time and my granny sells them, with her other son, who is my uncle, a farmer. The little piggies go to market. But there was a very PRETTY little piglet my granny wanted to keep, so she hid it from my uncle under her cushions! Nobody knew the piglet was there but when it got late my granny got SLEEPY and went to lie down. But she forgot the piglet was there and she is quite fat, so the piglet squealed when she lay on it, and jumped down and ran out of the room. And my gran chased him all round the house, while my uncle laughed and laughed. So they decided 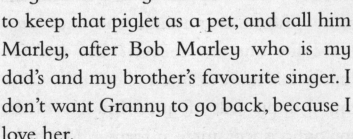 to keep that piglet as a pet, and call him Marley, after Bob Marley who is my dad's and my brother's favourite singer. I don't want Granny to go back, because I love her.

(Rosie didn't use SLEEPILY, she used SLEEPY, which is different, but the others didn't notice.)

Kitty's story

A long time ago, even before Mum and
Dad were invented, a WITCH lived in a
wood, and she liked to eat babies for her
dinner. But she couldn't find many in the
wood and so she had to go out and look
because she was getting very THIN. She
walked through the trees but it started to
RAIN, and she got very wet. She
stamped her foot ANGRILY and said,
'It's not fair, I don't want to get wet and
I don't want to get any thinner.' Just then
she saw a red apple on a tree and she
sang 'Yummy, yummy, yummy, some
food for my old tummy.' She got the
apple and took a bite . . . but this was a
good apple full of good magic. So the
witch turned into a nice lady who
looked just like Mum, and promised
never to eat any more babies. She stuffed
herself with crisps and chocolate and

lemonade and got very fat, until one day she had a baby herself and lived happily ever after.

Dad's shopping-list

Kitty thought that going shopping was the most boring thing in the whole world, next to playing rounders at school and tidying her room. When she was little she used to lie on the floor at the door of the supermarket and kick her heels and scream, 'Don't want to!'

When she was a little bit older, she once hid Mum's purse so they couldn't go out shopping, so Mum ran all round the house shouting, 'I can't find my purse!' and everybody got cross. Kitty's mum never found out what really happened.

Now Kitty knew she had to be a bit more grown-up, especially when Mum pointed out that if nobody went shopping they would all get very thin. Worse, in time their clothes would wear out and they would end up walking round with nothing on – which would be a bit chilly.

Still – she hated shopping. So, when one Saturday Dad told her to get her coat on and come out with him, her heart sank.

'Are we going to the park, Dad?' she asked, thinking that it was worth a try.

'Sorry, pet, here's our list of things to buy,' said Dad, waving it in the air.

'Can't you take Daniel?' whined Kitty.

'Dan's coming with us, and we're dropping him off at the sports centre for the new swimming club,' said Dad.

'It's not fair! Can't I stay here?' said Kitty.

'No you can't. I want to give Mum a bit of peace, now Tom's asleep,' said Dad.

'Don't be such a nuisance Kitty,' said

Daniel. 'Just be helpful, for once.'

'Boring goody-goody!' growled Kitty.

They set off, and soon they were in the High Street. Cars and buses roared by, and Kitty was already fed up. Dad and Daniel were chatting away, and she lagged behind feeling left out. When they got to the sports centre Daniel waved goodbye, but Kitty just gave him a dirty look because she thought he was lucky not to go shopping.

'Come on, KitKat,' said Dad, cheerfully.

First they went into a shop that sold everything for cars. Dad said he needed some de-icer, because winter was coming on – but of course he started to look at everything else in the shop.

'That's not on your list, Dad!' Kitty wailed when he picked up some paint and started to chat to the assistant about the best ways to touch up scratches.

'You're right, Kit, it isn't,' said Dad, and paid for the de-icer.

Next they went to a hardware store, which sold all sorts of things for the house and garden. Kitty thought it was probably the most boring shop in the world, because it was stuffed with dusters, dyes and doormats, plugs, paint-brushes and polishes, and so on.

Dad said he needed some nails and a new clothes line. But then a friend of his came in and they started to look at the tools that hung on the wall at the end of the shop.

'We need a new drill,' Dad explained.

'This one's good, and not a bad price,' said his friend.

'Dad! That's not on your list!' complained Kitty.

'You're right, Kit, it isn't,' Dad said, and

paid for the clothes line and nails.

The chemist was next door, and in they went to get a new bottle for Baby Tom. Dad seemed to take ages looking at the different ones. Then he picked up little tins of baby food and read the labels, and asked the lady which she thought was best. Kitty knew that was a waste of time because Thomas was still too young for solid food. Then Dad noticed a bib with blue rabbits all over it.

'Look, Kitty, isn't that nice? Do you think Tom would like it?' he asked.

'He's too little to even notice – and anyway, it's not on your list, Dad!' said Kitty sulkily.

'No, it's not, but Mum will be pleased,' Dad said as he paid for the bottle and the bib, and bought some disposable nappies as well.

'If you don't stick to the silly list we'll be out all day,' snapped Kitty.

When they went into the supermarket Kitty wanted to ride in the trolley like she used to, but Dad said she was too big. 'You can hold the list for me, if you like,' he added in a voice which made it sound as if she was a baby. Crossly, she took it – and groaned because it seemed so long.

At the biscuits section she left the list the shelf because she was looking at the chocolate fingers. When Dad discovered what she had done, he was irritated. He left her with the trolley while he went back to look. The list had disappeared.

'Perhaps we'd better go home then,' said Kitty hopefully.

'No chance! I can remember everything on it,' sighed Dad.

They bought onions, apples, bananas, carrots, sprouts, sausages, lamb chops, fruit yoghurts, digestive biscuits, tea bags, coffee . . . and lots of other boring things.

'Please get me some chocolate fingers,' whined Kitty. 'Please, Dad!'

'They aren't on the list,' said Dad.

There was a long queue at the check-out, and Kitty sighed and moaned. It made it worse when Dad put the de-icer, clothes line, nails, nappies, baby bottle and bib into a bag and told her she had to carry it. At last he had loaded two bags up with the food, and they walked out of the shop.

'Can we go home now?' asked Kitty.

'Why?'

'Because I'm bored, Dad!' shouted Kitty.

'Oh, are you indeed? Well, we've still got a couple more things to get.'

Kitty groaned.

On the way back they had to pass Kitty's favourite shop – which was a toy shop, of course. To her amazement Dad stopped outside and said they had to go in. 'I've got to get a pencil-case for Dan for school, and Mum thinks it's time Tom had a really good baby toy to get his little hands working.'

'So were those things on your list?' Kitty asked in a small voice.

'Yes, didn't you notice?' said Dad.

Kitty felt as if something cold had stuck in her stomach, and the weight of it was pulling the corners of her mouth down. She trailed after Dad, carrying her shopping-bag, and decided that when they got home she would be so naughty she would make *everybody* miserable – even the baby.

Kitty was so busy feeling sorry for herself she did not notice where Dad went or what he was doing. When they got to the till she noticed that he held the brightly coloured baby toy and the pencil-case – but also some Plasticene and a drawing book and a small box of coloured pencils.

Kitty's heart went jumpety-bump. Could it be . . . ? Were they for her?

Dad looked down at her with a smile. 'So you think we should stick to the shopping-list, do you, Kitty?'

'Er . . . yes, Dad.'

'Even when I decide to buy presents for a naughty girl who doesn't really deserve them?'

'Er . . . no, Dad.'

Dad ruffled her hair, paid, and they walked home together. Kitty felt very excited and couldn't stop saying thank you. She knew she would be busy for the rest of the day with her new things.

'Well,' said Dad, as he fished in his pocket for the front door key, 'are you going to tell Mum that shopping isn't boring after all?'

'No, Dad,' said Kitty with a grin. 'You always tell me to be truthful and the truth is – all shopping is boring, unless it's for ME!'

Melissa and the museum

'You've got to go, Kitty!' said Mum.

'No – I don't want to!' shouted Kitty.

'You promised me you'd be good today,' sighed Mum.

'But *you* promised you'd take me out! It's not fair!' shouted Kitty.

'I can't now.'

'Why not?'

'Because the health visitor is coming to check Tom. So Auntie Susan kindly offered to take you out instead.'

'I wish she hadn't,' muttered Kitty.

'Don't be so ungrateful,' snapped Mum. 'You'll have a lovely time with Melissa at the museum.'

Now, if there were two words which were going to send Kitty off to sleep they were 'Melissa' and 'Museum'. Daniel knew this and grinned. 'Melissa should be in a museum,' he laughed. 'Hey, Kit, maybe they'll take a fancy to her and put her in a glass case wearing her best dress.'

'Yeah, with a label on saying DINOSAUR GIRL,' grinned Kitty.

'Oh, you children are so mean,' sniffed Mum, turning away.

Just then the doorbell rang, and in a few seconds Kitty's dreaded cousin entered the room. She was dressed just as Kitty knew she would be. 'Like the fairy on the Christmas tree,' whispered Daniel.

Kitty was, of course, wearing her usual grubby clothes. It wasn't that Mum didn't bother to put clean ones out. It was just that the breakfast cereal, milk, butter and jam all seemed to want to stick to her clothes, no matter how hard she tried.

'You've got a hole in your lip, Kit,' Dad always said.

The truth was, even though Kitty didn't want to wear smart clothes like Melissa did, her cousin always made her *feel* silly, dirty and babyish. Just like now. Melissa looked Kitty up and down and asked, 'Are you going up to change, Kitty?' in her most superior voice.

'No, I'm not,' said Kitty.

'Are you looking forward to going to the museum?' asked Melissa.

'No, I'm not,' said Kitty.

'I am,' said Melissa sweetly.

'You would be,' muttered Kitty.

Mum was talking to Auntie Susan and

heard none of this – which was lucky for Kitty. And in a few minutes they said goodbye and set off for the town centre.

The truth was, Kitty was quite glad to be out of the house, because she was fed up with the baby crying and Daniel always having homework to do instead of playing with her. She knew, too, that

Auntie Susan would buy them delicious sandwiches and some sweets, because she was really very kind.

But Kitty could not help it; some little naughty imp seemed to get inside her head and make her sulky. Of course, Auntie Susan knew Kitty very well and took no notice. But Melissa always seemed to try to make it worse.

'You're very quiet today, Kitty,' she said, in that I'm-much-better-than-you voice Kitty hated.

'Dad says you should only talk when you've got something to say,' said Kitty.

'Oh, that *would* be dull!' smiled Auntie Susan.

The museum and art gallery was part of the town hall, and Kitty had never been there before. She always imagined museums to be old, dusty places, full of old, dusty things, with spiders in corners, and faded labels you couldn't read on things you didn't want to look at.

So her first surprise was at the entrance – because everything was bright and welcoming, and there was a big notice up announcing an exhibition of African art.

'First we'll look at the museum's normal display – all about the history of our town,' said Auntie Susan. 'Then we'll go and see if we like that exhibition. All right, girls?'

Kitty thought she sounded just like a teacher, and wanted more then ever to go home. But Melissa nodded and said, 'All right, Mummy.'

Kitty was very surprised by the first room. There were big posters on the walls telling how their town began as a tiny, tiny village, and how the Romans came, and how it got bigger, and so on.

The posters were easy to read – like lots of stories on the wall – and there were big pictures too, showing what it must have looked like.

Kitty thought she would have liked to have been there when the Romans came – as long as they were friendly.

'We learnt about them in school, Auntie Susan,' she said. 'They built good roads and things.'

'Look, there's part of a real Roman floor,' said Auntie Susan pointing. 'It's called a mosaic.'

Kitty thought the bit of floor was brilliant. It was made of hundreds of piece of pottery, all put together to make a picture. She could see a fish, some blue waves and part of a man with a beard, who was holding a thing like a garden fork. The label said he was the god of the sea.

'I'm going to make a mosaic when I get home,' she said, 'but I suppose I'll have to break some cups and plates to get the pieces!'

'Don't do that, Kitty – your Mum will never forgive me!' laughed Auntie Susan.

They walked on, and after a while Kitty noticed Melissa was very quiet. She didn't bother to read any of the stories on the walls, just glanced at them quickly then walked away. But Kitty found that she really liked looking at the things in cases – especially the thick rings, bracelets and necklaces that had been found near the town.

'Buried treasure!' she said. 'Look, Melissa.'

'Ugh — I'd rather have my butterfly brooch,' said Melissa.

After a while they wandered through to the room where the special exhibition was. The first thing they saw in the middle of the room was a huge black mask made from wood, all decorated with feathers and beads. Actually, it was a bit frightening. Kitty ran behind it, and made strange noises at Melissa.

'Woooo-oooo,' she went.

'Don't be silly, Kitty,' said Melissa nervously.

The room was full of wonderful things. There were lots more masks, and carved animals like monkeys, horses and bulls, and pottery bowls with wild patterns on them. She giggled at a funny model of a man holding a baby just as if it were a rugby ball.

'Looks like my dad!' she said.

Then there were axes and spears, and necklaces and cloaks, and strange statues. It all made Kitty think of faraway places and wish she could go. It was even better when somebody in the museum put on a tape of chanting and singing, which drifted down all around them from the speakers high on the walls.

'Look, Melissa, don't you like that great big pot? I wonder what they kept in it . . . ' Auntie Susan was saying. 'It's very old. Amazing it wasn't broken . . . '

'Yes, Mummy,' sighed Melissa, in a very dull voice.

Kitty couldn't believe it! She actually saw Auntie Susan frown at Melissa – who was always so good. To make matters worse, Melissa asked, 'Can we go home now, Mummy?'

'Goodness me, why?' asked Auntie Susan.

'Because I'm bored,' said Melissa, in a very spoilt voice.

'Oh,' said Auntie Susan.

She sounded so disappointed, Kitty felt sorry for her. Suddenly she thought it must be awful to arrange a treat, and then for someone to say it's boring . . . How babyish Melissa was!

'I don't want to go, Auntie Susan,' Kitty cried. 'I'm having a lovely time. I'm not bored!'

Melissa gave her a dirty look. In fact it would have been a *very* dirty look if her face had not been so pink and clean.

'Good girl!' said Auntie Susan.

It was so unusual for anyone to say that to Kitty she had to stop herself from turning round to see who her aunt was talking to!

'I thought we'd stay a bit longer, then go to the café for chicken sandwiches and ice-cream,' said Auntie Susan, 'but if Melissa really wants to go home . . .'

By this time Kitty was behind her cousin, and she could not stop herself. She pinched Melissa's arm, not too hard, just enough to let her know.

'Ow . . . I mean, how long before lunch then?' said Melissa.

'You want to stay?' asked Auntie Susan.

This time Kitty gave Melissa a tiny jab, and she said, 'Ow . . . didn't really mean I wanted to go.'

Kitty's aunt looked happy again led them through the last room where there were lots of baskets in piles, as well as a huge scary statue like a totem pole – and some stories on the walls about the tribes who had made them. Kitty read everything, and thought how much more fun it was to decide not to be bored.

Then they had their sandwiches, ice-cream and lemonade, and in the museum shop Auntie Susan bought them both a bookmark with the town crest on it, and a rubber and a pencil, too. Then she picked up a postcard of the big mask they had seen when they first went in.

'This is for you to stick up in your room, Kitty, because I know you were really interested,' she said.

When they got back to Kitty's house Mum opened the door. She looked worried.

'Was it all right?' she asked, giving

Auntie Susan a look. Kitty knew it meant, *was Kitty really naughty as usual*?

'We had a brilliant time, Mum,' said Kitty, as Auntie Susan bent down and put an arm round her.

'It was Kitty who was brilliant!' nodded her aunt.

Then Kitty was not sure which gave her the most pleasure – her mother's complete amazement, or Melissa's sulk.

First smile

'Now, Kitty, I want you to look after the baby,' said Mum.

'What!' cried Kitty.

'I said I need you to keep an eye on Tom.'

'Why me?' asked Kitty.

'Because there's nobody else in the house, Kitty!' said Mum in a very patient voice. 'And I really must spend a bit of time upstairs doing the bedrooms. I thought he had a little cough this morning, so I just want you to be in the room with him and tell me if he coughs again.'

'I can't,' said Kitty.

'Why not?'

'Because I won't know what to do,'

groaned Kitty.

Mum sighed and rolled her eyes to heaven. 'Kitty – for a start he's asleep. Then all I want you to do is draw or read, and just listen. If he wakes up and coughs, give me a shout. Now – is that too much to ask?'

'But I wanted to go to Will –'

'OH, KITTY!'

Kitty knew it was time to shut up. But as her mother walked crossly out of the room she muttered, 'Babies are boring.'

Mum turned round. 'Did you say something, Kitty?' she asked in a threatening voice.

'Er . . . I said baby's snoring,' said Kitty innocently.

'No he is not. Now don't be so silly,' Mum said, and left.

Kitty crept over to the carrycot that stood in the corner of the room, and peered in. Tom was fast asleep, just as Mum had said, all bundled up in his clothes and covers. All Kitty could see was the top of his head, like a little egg.

Kitty watched for a few moments, but he didn't move. So she went to turn on the TV, then stopped. It might wake 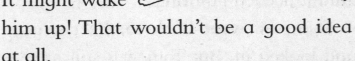 him up! That wouldn't be a good idea at all.

So she wandered around the living-room looking for something to do. Her books and toys were upstairs in her room, and Kitty didn't want to leave Tom in case Mum got cross.

She doodled for a while on a pad with Mum's best pen, then picked up a magazine and turned the pages. But it was full of pictures of silly film stars and people she had never heard of sitting by big swimming-pools and in very posh rooms – which Kitty thought was very boring.

She looked out of the window into the street, wondering why there were so many cars, and picked little curls of paint off the windowsill with her fingernails. She thought she'd better tell Dad it needed painting.

Then she went back to the carrycot and looked in. But Tom was still asleep. He hadn't moved at all. Kitty bent down to listen. There didn't seem to be a sound. Suddenly she felt worried. What if he wasn't breathing at all? What if . . . ?

Oh! At that moment he turned slightly in his sleep, and made a tiny noise, like a kitten. In fact it was so like a little sleepy mew it made Kitty smile, despite herself.

Now Kitty found herself wanting her baby brother to wake up. If he coughed she would have something to go and tell Mum, and then she could escape.

So, very, very gently she stretched out a finger and just touched Tom lightly on the tip of his nose. She knew her finger was cold – and sure enough, he seemed to feel it, because he made another little noise.

Just then Mum popped her head round the door. 'Is everything all right?' she asked.

'No – I'm bored,' said Kitty. She just couldn't help it.

'Too bad,' Mum said – and disappeared.

Kitty walked around the room again, picking up ornaments and putting them down, and wondering why grown-ups had so much silly stuff. She wouldn't, she decided; when she was old she would live with Mr Tubs in a big barn full of useful things like modelling clay, games and toys.

She daydreamed about how it must be great to have nobody to tell you what to do. You would be grown-up and yet still stay the same and want to play games . . . then she heard the little noise again.

She tiptoed to the carrycot, peered over the side – and got a shock. Two big blue eyes were looking at her. She stared at Baby Tom, and he stared back at her . . . and then his little round face started to pucker.

'Don't cry – please don't cry!' whispered Kitty.

Without thinking she waggled her fingers in a little wave, trying to turn Tom's attention from whatever it was that made him want to cry.

'Ga-ga-ga,' he said.

'What's that supposed to mean?' asked Kitty with a big smile.

Tom waved his two hands in the air, as if he was excited. They reminded Kitty of pictures she had seen of sea anemones with pink waving things sticking out on top.

'Ga-ga-ga-ga-ga-GA!' gurgled Tom.

Kitty put out a finger to touch his hand, and found herself grasped tightly by five little fat fingers. For some reason it really pleased her. It was as if the baby wanted to play.

'Oohh, who's a big, tough baby then? Who is?' she cooed.

They had a little tug of war, and Kitty giggled because her brother really was strong. She decided to see if he was ticklish too.

He was. He crumpled up as she tickled him under his chin (or rather chins) and all round his ears. He kicked his legs in the air and waved his arms about. Kitty laughed and laughed, and suddenly thought all this was rather fun.

'Do you like me, baby?' she whispered, and Tom made the happiest, gurgling, cooing noises she had ever heard.

Then – he smiled at her. It was a funny, toothless, wobbly smile, as if he was not sure how to do it. But it was a smile.

Kitty ran to the door. 'Mum! Mum!' she shouted. 'Come here, Mum!'

A worried face appeared at the top of the stairs. 'It's all right, Mum, he's not coughing or anything. But he *smiled*!'

Mum came running down. 'No he didn't, Kit – he's not learnt to smile yet. He must have a windy tummy.'

'He did smile – he did! At *me*!'

They went into the sitting-room. Mum picked Tom up and sat down with him on her lap, rubbing his back. Kitty knelt on the floor and let him take hold of her finger again. Then she wagged her head up and down and waved her captured finger about as if she was conducting an orchestra.

'Gheee–ghee–ghee,' said Tom, smiling really well now.

'Look, Mum!' said Kitty – and she saw that Mum had suddenly gone all soppy and bright-eyed, with a grin so big it split her face in two.

'His first smile,' she whispered in a voice like melted chocolate.

'And it was at me!' said Kitty proudly.

Somehow or other Mum managed to hug them both at once. 'Oh, Kitsy, that's 'cos he already knows you're the funniest girl in the whole world,' she said.

Mummy Kitty

Oh dear, it was one of those days. Dad and Daniel had gone out to a football match, which Kitty thought was not fair at all. She didn't want to go to the football match herself, but the sight of them in their scarves, all ready to have a good time, talking about boring old strikers and things like that – annoyed Kitty.

Then she couldn't find her crayons anywhere, and Mum said it was because her room was such a mess. 'Go and tidy it, Kitty,' she said crossly.

'No – that's boring!' said Kitty, and bounced out of the kitchen, slamming the door behind her.

She heard her Mum yell, 'KITTY!' but

chose to ignore her. She went upstairs, picked . Mr Tubs off her bedroom floor, pulled her duvet over her bed, and thought that would do. The truth was, her room was so untidy it wasn't nice to be in, but Kitty thought that sooner or later Mum would give in and tidy it for her. So that's what she was waiting for.

In fact, she thought as she wandered into the bathroom, it was about time Mum got tidying in there too. Kitty remembered she had pulled the bath towel on to the floor and left it there, and saw that when she cleaned her teeth she had smeared toothpaste on the basin. 'Messy,' she said aloud, and walked away.

I might as well go and visit William, since there's nothing happening here, Kitty thought, and quietly walked downstairs. She didn't want Mum to come upstairs and check her room. But when she was standing in the hall she heard a strange sound. She thought it came from the kitchen, but since the door was tightly closed she could not be sure.

Kitty listened. There it was again. Could it be Baby Tom? No – she knew he was in the sitting-room asleep, and this sound definitely came from the kitchen. It was a little snuffling noise that came and went. What could it be?

Very slowly Kitty turned the knob, and pushed open the door. Then she saw a sight which really horrified her. Mum was sitting at the kitchen table with her head in her hands – and she was crying.

Kitty thought the worst thing in the world was seeing a grown-up cry. Grown-ups aren't supposed to cry, they're supposed to make you feel better when *you* cry.

Once she had seen a teacher at school with teary eyes, but she didn't know why. And once she had seen Dad cry, years ago when his mum, the granny she hardly remembered, had died. Mum cried more often, sometimes at films on the television (but that didn't count) and once or twice when she'd had an argument with Dad.

This was different somehow. Mum looked – sort of – helpless.

'What's the matter, Mum?' asked Kitty.

'N-n-nothing,' sniffed Mum.

'Yes there is,' said Kitty. 'Please tell me.'

Mum took a big breath and turned to

Kitty. Her face was all red and streaky. She looked almost cross as she said, 'Do you really want to know? All right, Kitty, I think you're old enough to hear how I feel.'

Kitty nodded.

Mum went on, 'I just get so fed up being in the house all day. There's so much to do because of Tom and the rest of you, and I just find it all gets me down, and you remember I gave up my job?' Kitty nodded. 'Well I wanted to have Tom – of course I did – but I miss my job and I just – I just get . . . ' She started to wail, 'I just get so tired and *bored* all day. I can't bear it!'

'Oh, Mum,' said Kitty in a very small voice.

'I'm sorry,' whispered Mum. 'It's not your fault. I just wish I had some time for myself.'

Kitty had a brainwave. 'Mum! Remember you used to love to lie on your bed reading a good book, with one of those funny mud masks on for your skin?'

Mum nodded. 'Oh, when did I have have time for that?' she muttered.

'Today!' said Kitty.

She started to heave her mum up from the table. She was all floppy, and did not try to resist. Kitty pulled and pushed her

towards the kitchen door. 'Go on!' she said, 'I want you to go and hide in your room, and have some time to yourself, and leave everything to me!'

'What? Oh, I can't,' Mum protested.

'Yes, you can! Oh, please try . . . just for me!' said Kitty.

She told her mother she would look after Tom and tidy up, and to her surprise there were no more protests. Mum must be really tired and miserable to give in, Kitty thought, as she watched her go upstairs. 'Don't worry — I'll tell you if I need you,' she called.

Kitty was determined to prove she could do this, so she started to work harder than she had ever worked in her life. She whizzed around the kitchen, cleaning it up, then ran into the sitting-room. She decided to pretend she was a robot somebody had programmed to move really fast, picking up newspapers, plumping the cushions, and so on.

Then it was dusting, and she was quite shocked to see how much dust there was on the mantelpiece. That was because she had never looked before. Poor Mum, she thought.

When she had finished she took a deep breath and went upstairs to tackle her own room and the bathroom. What a mess! she thought, but didn't stop.

Round and round she went, doing what she could to make things look better. She found her crayons under her bed, as well as a couple of other things she had lost. It all seemed to take ages, despite her speed. She even made Daniel's bed, although she thought how lazy and horrible he was not to make it himself. But a thought struck her. 'Maybe we're all lazy and horrible, and

don't think of Mum enough,' she said
to herself.

Then Kitty remembered the baby and
ran downstairs again. She went into the
sitting-room and very, very carefully
picked Thomas out of his carrycot. She
sniffed the air. 'Oh no!' She sniffed again,
a bit closer to his bottom. 'Oh, you've
pooed your nappy, Tom – and just when
I'm looking after you!'

Kitty didn't want to disturb Mum, but
all the baby equipment was in her
bedroom. So Kitty held the baby tightly

and went upstairs. Mum was lying on her bed, with a pink face pack on, reading a book – just as Kitty had told her to. She looked so funny she made Kitty laugh.

'Now stay there, Mum,' Kitty said, 'because I'm going to change Tom's nappy.'

'Oh, but you can't, love!' said Mum.

'Yes I can,' said Kitty. She was rather enjoying bossing Mum about.

She put Tom down on his back (just as she had seen Mum do so many times) and set to work.

'Pooh!' she said.

'It certainly is!' said Mum

Then Kitty said, 'Double-pooh!' Then, 'Yuk!' Then, 'Ugh!'

But she still did it – whilst Mum looked on, cracking her mud mask with a big smile.

At last Tom was fresh and clean and smelling of talcum powder. Mum held out her arms and Kitty put him in them. 'He can go back to sleep here with me,' said Mum softly. 'Thank you, KittyKat.'

'Wait till you see what I've done all over the house!' said Kitty proudly.

'Thank you, KittyKat,' said Mum again, as if she had forgotten all her words.

They looked at each other for a moment, then Kitty felt embarrassed. 'If you don't mind, Mum, I think I'll go and have a rest,' she said.

Back in her own room, Kitty looked around, feeling very pleased with herself. It was so clean and tidy she wanted to be in there. She could suddenly think of lots of things she wanted to do. But first she lay down on the bed, next to her bear.

'Well, Mr Tubs, I'm exhausted, you hear me? I've had all the cleaning and tidying to do, and can you imagine what that's like?'

Mr Tubs looked at her sympathetically, but said nothing.

'You know, it isn't easy when there's so much to do and no one to help you. Can you imagine how tiring and boring it is, with a house *and* a baby to look after?'

Mr Tubs said nothing.

'As for the dirty nappies – oh dear! Now, you've got to make me a huge promise, Mr Tubs. Will you?'

The bear seemed to nod and wait.

Kitty cuddled him close and said, 'Just never, ever, *ever* call me Mummy! OK?'